He's the Prince of Pranks!

PRINCE JAKE

Dungeon of Doom

FOR HANNAH, TOM AND HOLLY
POWELL, WITH LOTS OF LOVE
S.M.

FOR MY GOOD FRIEND,
BRIAN BENSON
M.B.

ORCHARD BOOKS
338 Euston Road, London NW1 3BH
Orchard Books Australia
Level 17/205 Kent St, Sydney, NSW 2000

First published in 2008 by Orchard Books
First paperback publication in 2009
Text © Sue Mongredien 2008
Illustrations © Mark Beech 2008

The rights of Sue Mongredien to be identified as the author
and Mark Beech to be identified as the illustrator of this work
have been asserted by them in accordance with
the Copyright, Designs and Patents Act, 1988.
A CIP catalogue record for this book is available from the British Library.

ISBN HB 978 1 40830 280 4
ISBN PB 978 1 84616 617 4

HB 1 3 5 7 9 10 8 6 4 2
PB 1 3 5 7 9 10 8 6 4 2

Printed in Great Britain by
CPI Antony Rowe, Chippenham, Wiltshire

Orchard Books is a division of Hachette Children's Books
an Hachette Livre UK company.
www.hachettelivre.co.uk

PRINCE JAKE

He's the Prince of Pranks!

JAKE

Dungeon of Doom

SUE MONGREDIEN   MARK BEECH

ORCHARD BOOKS

CHAPTER ONE

It was a Friday lunchtime in the castle of Morania, and everyone around the royal dining table was deep in thought.

Prince Jake was plotting. He and Prince Ned had been trying to catch rats last night, down by the dungeons. Jake was really hoping they could get one and sneak it into Princess Petunia's four-poster bed. It would be so funny!

Prince Ned was excited. He couldn't wait

for PE that afternoon. The captain of the Moranian national football team, Hat-trick Haywood, was visiting the castle to give the royal children a special training session. How cool was that?!

Princess Petunia was daydreaming. She was imagining herself scoring the winning goal in the annual Toffs versus Town polo match tomorrow. She and her mum were in the Toffs team, along with "Gorgeous"

George Barrington, the Duke of Bentley's son. "Oh, Petunia," she hoped George would say. "You were fabulous!"

King Nicholas was licking his lips. Would it be really greedy of him to have another spoonful of roast potatoes? "Well, I *am* King, after all," he muttered to himself, signalling to Boris, the butler, that he would like more. "And kings get to do whatever they want!"

Queen Caroline was fretting. She'd lost her best bracelet, which had been in the Moranian royal family for years. It was solid silver, and clipped together with a little hinge. She always wore it for polo matches as a lucky charm, but it seemed to have vanished.

"Boys, have you seen my silver bracelet anywhere?" she said at that moment, gazing over the dining table at her sons.

Prince Jake pretended to be chewing a tough bit of roast goose, while he thought about what to say. He certainly wasn't going to tell the truth! If his mum knew that he and Ned had been using her precious bracelet as part of a rat lasso they'd made, she'd have a right royal fit!

Prince Ned, who was younger than Jake and a lot less sneakier, piped up. "We were playing with it near the dungeons," he said, "and—"

8

Jake kicked him under the table and shot him a warning look. "He means, we were taking it to be polished for you, and went past the dungeons," he fibbed, in his most innocent voice. "And—"

Prince Ned let out a snigger. "And then Jake got scared because we thought we heard the ghost, and we ran away, and—"

"I was not scared!" Jake interrupted indignantly. "YOU were scared, more like. And anyway, it was only that door banging that made me jump a bit. There's no way I'm scared of ghosts."

"There isn't a ghost down there anyway," King Nicholas said, through a mouthful of potato. "That's just a silly story."

Princess Petunia shuddered. "Well, you wouldn't catch me going down there," she said firmly. "Ugh! It's all spidery and spooky and cold."

"So, what happened to my bracelet?" the Queen put in.

"Wimp!" Jake scoffed at his sister.

"I'm NOT a wimp!" Petunia raged, flicking a sprout off Jake's nose with perfect aim.

Mrs Pinny, the housekeeper, was at the table, stacking plates to take out. "Me and the other girls are always hearing ghostly howls and moans from that middle dungeon," she said. "I'm just glad that the key is lost, so the spooks can't get out." She shivered, and her huge bottom wobbled like twin blancmanges as she left the room.

"WHERE IS MY BRACELET?" the Queen
bellowed, making everyone jump.

"Oh," said Jake. "Well, er…"

"I haven't got it," Ned said, holding up his
empty palms for all to see.

"Sorry, Mum," Jake said. "I think we must
have left it down there."

The Queen frowned. "Well, kindly go
and fetch it," she snapped. "You know
how special that bracelet is to me. And
next time, ask before you help yourself
to my things."

11

"OK, OK," Jake sighed.

"Here's your dessert – double chocolate mousse," Mrs Pinny said, re-entering the room with a large silver dish.

Jake stared at it, licking his lips. Yum! The royal chef made the most fabulous chocolate mousse ever. Today, he had even iced a chocolate crown on the top, and decorated it with tiny silver balls.

"*Now*, please, boys," the Queen said.

"But what about pudding?" Ned protested, his gaze not leaving the silver dish. Mrs Pinny was plunging a spoon into the mousse with a loud, wet, squelch.

The Queen raised her eyebrows. "We'll save you some," she said. "IF you're quick. Now go!"

Jake hesitated, his eye on the silver spoon in Mrs Pinny's hand.

"LOADS for me, please," Petunia said sweetly, then stuck her tongue out at Jake. "You know, I'm so hungry, I'll probably have at least three bowlfuls. And all the decorations..."

Jake and Ned bolted for the door at once. "You'll get SPOTS if you do," Jake bellowed at her as an after-thought. "And then Georgie-Boy will NEVER fancy you!"

The boys raced through the Great Hall and down the basement steps towards the dungeons. Down in the corridor, the bracelet was lying on the stone floor where it had been abandoned.

Jake stuffed it in his pocket and was just about to turn and go back for his pudding when he stopped outside the middle dungeon and gave the old wooden door an experimental push. It didn't budge. He bent down to look at the keyhole, noticing for the first time that the rusty metal plate around it was shaped like a dragon's head.

Jake couldn't resist bending down and peeping through it but he could see nothing but darkness. How he wished he could have a look at what was inside the dungeon, especially after what Mrs Pinny had said about hearing ghostly howls and moans!

"Woooooooaaaaahhhhh!" came a blood-curdling cry behind him just then. Jake's heart almost stopped and he whirled around...to see Ned doubled over in fits of laughter.

"Got you there!" Ned chortled. "Should have seen your face! So you ARE scared of ghosts, after all!"

Jake glared at his little brother. "I am not," he said crossly. "I'm not scared of ANYTHING!"

CHAPTER TWO

The princes ran back to the dining hall, and Jake gave the bracelet to his mum, who frowned and began polishing the dirt off it with her napkin.

To Jake's relief, there was still plenty of mousse left, and he sighed happily as Mrs Pinny dished up a generous bowlful for him. "Yum," Jake said, tucking in with gusto. "Just what I need to fill me up before PE. I can't believe Hat-trick

Haywood's going to give us a lesson!"

The Queen looked rather surprised. "Oh! Didn't I say? I've told him not to bother coming in after all," she said.

"What?" Jake spluttered, dropping his golden spoon in shock. "Not coming?"

The Queen shook her head. "I need Petunia to practise her polo this afternoon, before the game tomorrow," she explained. "I didn't think it was worth Mr Haywood coming all this way when you won't all be there. I'll rearrange it for another time."

Jake sighed. No Hat-trick Haywood? No penalty shoot-out? Gutted! "What are me and Ned going to be doing, then?"

"Well, I thought you could have a bit of a kick-around with your father instead," Queen Caroline said.

"Un-lucky," Petunia tittered.

King Nicholas, who had been concentrating on scraping the very last bits of mousse from his bowl, looked up in dismay. "What? Me?" he said. "Do I have to?"

"Yes," the Queen said sternly. "You've got to set a good example to the nation, Nicholas. You've just eaten fifteen roast potatoes and five helpings of chocolate pudding. No one wants a big fat wobbly king on the throne."

The King slapped his large belly. "Muscle, this is," he said. "Solid muscle!"

"Solid lard, you mean," Jake muttered under his breath.

Half an hour later, Jake and Ned were playing keepy-uppies on the royal lawn when a big fat wobbly king in a too-tight football kit strode towards them, thighs jiggling with each step.

"He's got to be joking," Jake murmured to Ned, trying not to laugh out loud.

"How long do you give those shorts, before they split?" Ned giggled in reply.

"Five minutes," Jake said, eyeing the straining seams on his dad's large bottom.

"There's no way they'll last that long,"
Ned replied.

"Right, lads!" the King said, wibbling and
wobbling his way over. "Shall I be goalie?"

"No way, that's not fair," Jake said.
"You're nearly as wide as the goal, Dad.
We'll never be able to score past you."

The King ignored him. "Let's go over to
the football pitch," he said. "Your mum will
go bananas if the ball goes in any of her
rose bushes."

Jake hoofed the ball up the lawn and started running after it. "Come on, then, Dad," he shouted. "Tackle me!"

"No problem!" the King called, huffing and puffing after him. "Here I come!"

"We can tell, the ground's shaking," Ned joked, dodging nimbly in front of him as they all ran across the lawn. He barged into Jake, who barged him back, both jostling for the ball.

"Keep up, Dad!" Jake shouted, just getting to the ball before his brother. He glanced over his shoulder and saw the King, purple in the face, stopping and bending over to catch his breath. Then came a loud *Rrrrrriiiip!*

Both boys burst out laughing, and Ned checked his watch. "Two minutes exactly," he chuckled. "I win!"

"Blasted shorts!" the King fumed, trying to peer over his shoulder to see the damage.

"Cheap, shoddy material! They'll be losing the royal crest, all right!"

He turned to stomp back to the castle, and the boys could see a flash of bright red underpants through the ripped seam.

Jake was laughing so hard, he completely miskicked the ball, sending it wide of the goal, straight into a hedge. "Oops," he spluttered. "I'll just get that."

Jake sprinted over to the hedge, and crouched down to tug out the ball. As his fingers curved around it, he felt something cold on the ground too, beside the ball. Jake wondered what it was – it felt hard and thin, like some kind of metal stick – and he pulled it out with the ball, his curiosity building.

His eyes widened as he realised what the metal stick thing was. A key! An old-looking iron key, blackened with age. He turned it over, wondering which lock it fitted, and how it had ended up under the hedge.

Then his heart skipped a beat as he noticed that the top of the key was shaped like a dragon's head...and he remembered where he'd seen another dragon's head just like it.

At that moment there were footsteps behind him and Prince Ned appeared. "Hey, what's that?" he asked.

Jake grinned. Never mind Hat-trick Haywood. This football lesson was turning out way better than he'd hoped! He held up his find. "This," he said dramatically, "is the key to the haunted dungeon!"

CHAPTER THREE

Prince Ned's eyes grew very wide as he
stared at it. Then he raised an eyebrow.
"So, you probably want to check out the
ghost for yourself now," he said cheekily.
"Cos you're not scared of anything,
are you?"

"Too right I'm not!" Jake replied.

"So what do you reckon – ghost-hunting
tonight after dark?" Ned asked.

Jake hesitated. All of a sudden, the idea

of creeping around a haunted dungeon in darkness wasn't quite so appealing. But there was no way he wanted to lose face in front of his little brother. Especially after all the boasting he'd done about not being scared! "No worries," he blustered in his most confident voice. "I can't wait to see that ghost. Bring it on!"

After PE, the boys and Petunia had a History lesson with the royal governess, Ms Prudence, who was also known (to Jake, anyway) as the Prune. "We're going to continue with our project on your very own Royal Family today," she began, "studying some of the history surrounding this castle. Now—"

Jake put his hand up. "Ms Prune – I mean, Ms Prudence, could you teach us about the royal ghost?" he asked.

"Yeah, what's the story?" Ned put in.

"Did somebody die in the dungeon? Is that who haunts it?"

The Prune pushed up her spectacles. "Well," she said, perching on the edge of her desk. "It's quite an interesting tale, actually…"

Jake winked at Ned. Result! Once the Prune started on one of her stories, you could often write off the rest of the lesson.

"Now, nobody has actually seen a ghost – and if you ask me, such things don't exist, anyway," the Prune began primly, "but some of the more…fanciful members of staff believe that the dragon dungeon is haunted by…"

"The dragon dungeon?" Petunia echoed, wrinkling her nose. "Why is it called that?"

The Prune looked surprised at the question.

"My dear, have you never looked at the keyholes of the dungeons?" she asked. "One has a lion symbol on it, and another an eagle. And the middle dungeon has the symbol of a dragon on its keyhole. That was where the worst traitors were sent, as punishment. All the most horrible torture equipment was kept in there, so the stories go."

Jake felt a shiver down his spine. It was pretty grim, thinking about people being tortured and dying in the dragon dungeon, right here in the castle. He slipped a hand into his trouser pocket and his fingers closed around the cold key in there. He was already starting to have second thoughts about being so rash earlier, and saying he wasn't afraid of visiting the haunted dungeon. All this talk of torture and death was making him feel even worse!

"It is said that the dragon dungeon is haunted by the ghost of Earl Jeremiah, who was tortured there over five hundred years ago," the Prune began.

31

"Tortured to death?" Ned put in, an eager light in his eyes. "Was it really gruesome and gory?"

The Prune nodded. "Sadly, yes," she replied. "The Earl had been accused of stealing some of the King's best silver and selling it abroad. He was put to death for being a traitor, even though he denied any wrongdoing, right to his last breath."

"Probably a liar, as well as a thief," Petunia said, checking her lipgloss in a compact mirror. "Ms Prudence, do you think Frosted Pink suits me?"

The Prune gave her a disapproving look. "Mirror away, please, Petunia," she said. "There's a portrait of Earl Jeremiah in the Royal Gallery, if you're that interested," she went on, turning back to the boys.

Jake looked up, sensing the chance of a skive out of the classroom. "Oh, we are," he said quickly. "Can you show it to us, Miss?"

The Prune seemed overjoyed to hear the keen note in Jake's voice. He was never usually so interested in her history lessons. "Of course!" she beamed. "No time like the present. Bring your notebooks with you, in case you want to jot down any details."

The Prune led them out of the schoolroom, down the North Tower steps, and into the East Wing of the castle. The Royal Gallery was a boring place, Jake thought, full of oil paintings of snooty-faced dead royals, all looking down their noses at him. Today, though, he couldn't help

33

feeling a nervous prickle of excitement
at the thought of seeing a portrait of
the man who might now be the
dungeon ghost!

"Here we are," the Prune said a few
minutes later. She pointed up to a large
portrait of a black-haired man posing
with a wolfhound, which gazed adoringly
up at him.

"Looks a bit of a misery-guts," Petunia sniffed.

"You probably would too, if you were suspected of treason," Jake pointed out.

Petunia stuck her nose in the air. "Aren't there any pictures of the Barringtons in here?" she asked, flouncing away before Ms Prudence could even answer.

Jake stared at the picture. The Earl's eyes were dark and rather forbidding, and he had a stern set to his mouth. Jake turned his head away, suddenly rather fearful of the Earl's serious face.

Ned elbowed him in the ribs. "Looking forward to hanging out with him in the dungeon later?" he asked.

Jake glared. He wished his little brother would shut up about going to the dungeon! "Course I am," he fibbed. "I can't wait!"

That evening, Prince Jake was rather quiet. Partly because he was thinking about having to go into the haunted dungeon. Partly because he couldn't get a word in, with his sister wittering on about the polo match non-stop.

"I'm so nervous, but I'm so excited too," she gushed, as the royal family sat in one of the sitting rooms, watching a film together.

"I just wish I had a special lucky charm, like you and your bracelet, Mum, something to bring me good luck."

"You won't need any luck, dear," King Nicholas said from his plush red armchair, without taking his eyes off the TV. On screen, a group of space rangers were exploring a new planet. The TV was so huge, the people on it looked life-size. "Ooh!" he added, sitting forwards suddenly. "Don't go into that cave, guys!"

37

"The aliens are totally going to mangle them," Prince Jake said gleefully.

"How about your gold necklace with the solitaire diamond?" the Queen suggested to Princess Petunia.

Petunia shook her head. "I was wearing that last time I saw George," she said. "He'll think I've only got one piece of jewellery if I wear it again!"

"He'll think you've only got one brain cell if you bang on about jewellery like that, too," Jake muttered.

Petunia overheard him and scowled. "One brain cell? Well, that's one more than you've got," she retorted.

"Quiet, I can't hear the film," the King growled. "Look, he's just about to get eaten by the alien spider thing!"

"Oh, what can I have as my lucky charm?" Petunia wailed dramatically, clasping her blonde head in her hands.

Jake grinned, his dad's words suddenly giving him an idea. The room they were in was in the oldest, crumbliest bit of the castle and, if he was lucky, he'd be able to find just what he needed for his big sister...

He slipped off the sofa and went to the far corner of the room, where it was dark and a bit dusty. Then he groped around on the floor behind the heavy velvet curtains and... Aha! Excellent! The biggest, most dangly-legged spider in the whole castle, he reckoned!

"I've just thought of the perfect thing for you to wear tomorrow, Petunia," he said in his fakest nice-brother voice. He got to his feet carefully, the huge spider enclosed within his cupped hands.

"Oh yeah? Shock me with your brilliance," Petunia said sarcastically, without even bothering to look at him.

Jake went over to the sofa and with a deft, well-practised movement, pulled out the neck of Petunia's top and dropped the spider straight down her back. "There!" he said. "Spiders are really lucky, you know!"

The scream that followed was enough to wake every ghost in Morania.

"Aaaargh! Jake! I hate you!" Petunia shrieked, scrabbling to get the spider out of her clothes. "And if we lose the game tomorrow, it's going to be ALL YOUR FAULT!"

👑 👑 👑

"She's totally going to get you back, you know," Prince Ned warned later that night, as he and Prince Jake got ready for bed. "There's no way she'll let you get away with it."

Jake shrugged. "'S'all right," he said. "I'll live with it." Besides, he thought privately, nothing Petunia could chuck at him could possibly be as bad as having to come face to face with the ghost of scary-looking Earl Jeremiah.

He glanced out of his bedroom window. It was pitch-black outside, with just a few stars sprinkling the sky. As he watched, the clouds slid away, and a full moon shone. Jake shivered, feeling apprehensive. Oh, great. It would have to be a full moon tonight, wouldn't it? There'd probably be a werewolf roaming around the dungeon as well as the ghost, knowing his luck!

Jake was starting to feel sick with nerves at the thought of going in there on his own. Why, oh why, had he ever bragged that he wouldn't be scared?

Ned was looking at him. "You're not... You're not thinking of chickening out, are you?" he asked, followed by a raucous burst of clucking.

Jake shook his head crossly. His kid brother was getting too cheeky by half! "Of course not!" he said. "I'm not a chicken! In fact, what are we waiting for? Let's just go and do it now, before Mum and Dad come up to say goodnight."

Ned raised his eyebrows. "If you're sure…?"

Jake nodded. "I'm sure. Let's go."

The two boys padded downstairs as quietly as they knew how, not wanting Mrs Pinny or Boris, or any of the other members of staff, to spot them. Then they crept down the basement steps to the dungeons. It was dark, and the stone floor was cold under their bare feet. Jake switched his torch on, wishing he'd thought to wear his dressing gown. But if he turned back now, Ned would only think he was making excuses, and would make chicken noises at him again. And he definitely didn't want that.

44

Jake's fingers felt trembly around the key as they approached the dragon dungeon. He found himself hoping that the lock would have seized up with age, and he wouldn't be able to open the door. Or maybe it would be rusted over? Oh, please let it be rusted over!

With a thumping heart, Prince Jake put the key in the keyhole. It fitted

perfectly. He turned it, and it made
a dreadful grating noise, but then
there came a telltale click. The door
was unlocked.

Jake and Ned looked at each other.
"So I'll go in there, have a look around,
then come back out again," Jake said.
"Right?"

"Right," Ned agreed.

Here goes nothing, Jake thought, his mouth dry. The door gave a loud creak as he pushed it open, then Jake stepped inside the haunted dungeon.

CHAPTER FOUR

The door slammed shut behind him. "Say hello to the ghosts for me!" Ned shouted.

Jake stood still for a moment, shining his torch around the darkness. It was very cold in the dungeon, and it smelled damp and musty. He shivered as the torchlight fell on an old wooden torture rack. Was that where Earl Jeremiah had been stretched, until he begged for mercy? It was a horrible thought.

He swung the torch up across the wall
and saw two iron rings fixed to the
brickwork, and a length of old chain. He
grimaced. Was that where Earl Jeremiah
had hung, chained up like a dog, until his
wrists were raw with the pain?

Something scuttled across his bare foot,
and it was all he could do to stop himself
screaming out loud. Ugh! What was that?
A spider? A cockroach? Or something
worse? Were there any rats living in this
dungeon? What if one of them bit him,

sinking its great yellow teeth right into his toes?

Jake wrapped his arms around himself, feeling very cold and wishing he was tucked up in bed, warm and sleepy. He should never have said he'd do this! If only he hadn't found the stupid key!

He shone his torch over the stone floor. There were thick cobwebs in the corners, and an old bucket, and some kind of metal dish...but no sign of any ghosts.

Very slowly, Jake let out his breath, feeling hugely relieved. No ghosts. Not one. So the dungeon wasn't haunted, after all. In fact, he realised, as his heart rate began to slow, it wasn't even that scary. It was just a dark, cold, musty old room, that was all. So he'd stand here for a few minutes, then go back to meet Ned at the door. Then he could go to bed, a hero in his brother's eyes for braving the dungeon!

In fact, Jake thought, brightening now that he had the key, there were all sorts of ace things he could do with the dragon dungeon. He could definitely trick Petunia into coming down here, and lock her in to scare her witless. And maybe he could make it his own secret hideout, where he could stash things he didn't want his mum to see, or…

Suddenly, Jake's heart almost stopped. His eyes widened. What was that?

Something was shimmering in the corner. He stared through the darkness, as a ghostly white shape began appearing in the gloom. Two eyes, a pointed nose, four legs…

Jake stepped back, his skin prickling into goosebumps as a ghostly dog appeared right before his eyes. It was the wolfhound from Earl Jeremiah's portrait!

Jake stared in horror. Suddenly, the dungeon seemed colder than ever. The ghostly wolfhound sniffed the air, and Jake could see its ghostly nostrils twitching as it caught his scent. And then the wolfhound turned to look at him for a long, long moment, before tipping its head back and howling a dreadful howl.

"ARRROOOOOOOOO!"

Jake was frozen to the spot in terror. He was dimly aware of a scrabbling noise somewhere behind him, and voices.

"Hey! Give that back!" That was Ned, shouting at someone.

"No way!" That was Petunia, with a gloating laugh.

The dog stared at Jake, its eyes luminous.

"G-g-good doggy," Jake croaked, his voice trembling. "N-n-nice doggy!"

Then there came a hammering on the other side of the door, and Petunia's voice again. "I've got the key, Jake, and I've locked you in – let's call it payback for that spider," she shouted.

"No!" Jake cried. "Petunia! No! Let me out!"

"What's the magic word?" Petunia cooed.

"PLEASE!" Jake bellowed, not able to take his eyes off the ghost dog.

There was a pause. "Hmmm…" Petunia

said. "Actually, I think I'll let you out in
the morning – if you do some MAJOR
grovelling and begging, that is. Oh, and if
you haven't already been scared to death,
of course!" She laughed, as if she'd just said
the funniest thing ever. "Sweet dreams!"

"Petunia, please!" Jake yelled
desperately. "Let me out! There really
is a ghost in here!"

Petunia laughed again. "Like I'm
going to fall for that one!" she sneered.
"Night night!"

"Give it BACK!" Ned cried, his voice growing fainter. He was chasing her along the corridor, Jake realised in dismay. Which meant that now he was all alone down here. All alone, apart from the ghost dog, that was.

The wolfhound trotted across the room. Jake could see its ghostly tongue hanging out of its mouth and its enormous sharp teeth.

"N-n-nice doggy," he stuttered again. *Could a ghost actually kill you?* he wondered. *Could you really be scared to death?*

CHAPTER FIVE

The ghost dog came right up to Jake and
looked at him questioningly. Then
it pushed its nose into Jake's hand.

Jake shuddered. The dog's nose was as
cold as ice. "W-w-what do you want?"
he asked.

The dog trotted away from Jake, and
then looked back over its shoulder at him.

"You want me to follow you?" Jake said
in surprise.

The dog went a little further away, and looked back again at Jake. Jake followed, too scared to think straight.

The dog led Jake to the far corner of the dungeon where he saw a pile of roughly stacked bricks. The dog nosed at the bricks, then gazed back at Jake and whined.

Jake looked at the dog, unsure of what to do. The dog nosed at the bricks again, then gave a sharp bark.

"You want me to do something?" Jake asked nervously. He picked up a brick. It felt damp and crumbly in his fingers.

The dog barked again, and made a scrabbling motion at the bricks.

"You want me to…move them?" Jake ventured. "OK." He put the brick down behind him, then took another couple off the pile. Then he moved a couple more – and gasped.

Behind where the bricks had lain, he
could now see a hole that had been cut
unevenly in the wall. Jake crouched down
and shone his torch into the hole. Then
he gasped again. No way! Was that really
a secret tunnel?

The dog bent down to squeeze itself into
the tunnel and gave a short bark.

"We're going along there?" Jake asked.
He was starting to feel more excited
than scared now that the dog didn't
seem interested in biting or attacking him.

Wait till he told his brother about this!

Jake got down on all fours and crawled into the tunnel behind the dog. The wolfhound's tail shimmered in front of him, like a strange ghostly light, and Jake followed it, hardly able to believe what was happening. Where was the dog taking him? Where did the tunnel lead?

Jake's heart sank as an awful thought hit him. Could it be a trick? Would the ghostly Earl be waiting for him at the end of the tunnel, with a huge ghostly sword?

Jake gulped, wondering if he should turn back. But just then, the tunnel started to go upwards, and suddenly Jake could feel fresh, cold air. He guessed they were about to come outside into the open – but where?

The wolfhound gave another short bark and then disappeared from Jake's view. Jake could see the stars and moon above his head – thank goodness! – and squirmed out of the tunnel after the dog.

He stood up to find himself in the middle of a thick shrubbery. "We must be somewhere in the garden," he muttered, gazing over the tops of the bushes. He could see the moon glinting off the moat a little way to his left, and the west wing of the castle just behind him.

Wow! A secret tunnel from the dungeon! How cool was that?

He turned around to see if the dog was still there and realised it was scrabbling at the ground with its ghostly pale paws.

"What is it? What have you got there?" Jake asked, bending down to see. He used a stone to scrape away the earth – and

then almost fell over in excitement.
Something was buried there. Something
shiny. Something silver!

Jake dug away at the ground, his mind
racing at what he might find beneath the
surface. Some adventure this was turning
out to be!

His fingers struck something hard, and
he cleared away the damp soil to reveal
a box with a silver crest on the top. He
pulled it out in excitement, his fear
completely gone now. "Is this what you
wanted me to—?" he began, but his voice
faltered as he saw the ghost dog vanishing
before his eyes. "Thank you," Jake said to
the cold night air after a moment.
"Thanks for helping me escape."

He pushed the lid off the box and shone
his torch inside. A yellowed piece of
parchment lay on top, with sloping
black handwriting on it.

His heart pounding, Jake read the words:

To the one who finds this box, know this:
Earl Jeremiah was a good man. He did
not steal from the King. It was I, Robert
of Millfield, who took the treasures.
I hoped to journey across the sea, to sell
them and make my fortune, but my horse
was struck lame the same night, and
I feared that I was being punished by the
angry gods. I sent word to the Earl that
I would dig a tunnel down to him, to help
him escape, but by the time the tunnel was
complete, he was already dead. His blood
will forever be on my conscience.

I am filled with remorse. I did wrong.
I hope that one day these treasures will be
found, and the Earl's name will be cleared.

Signed on this day, 16th May, 1808
Robert West, of Millfield

Jake sat back on his heels, his mind trying to take it all in. Then he remembered the box, and shone his torch inside. He gaped as he saw a huge hoard of coins, a dagger in a scabbard and... His eyes widened in surprise. A second silver bracelet, just like the one his mum loved!

Jake picked up the box and ran towards the entrance of the castle. He could hardly wait to show Ned this little lot!

CHAPTER SIX

Prince Ned was outside the dungeon door, heaving and pushing against it with all his might, when Prince Jake ran down the corridor. Ned's eyes nearly fell out of his head when he saw his brother hurrying towards him. "Where did you come from? How did you get out?" he asked.

Jake grinned, but before he could answer there was a clattering of footsteps and along the corridor from the other direction came the King, Queen and Princess Petunia. Petunia looked sulky. The Queen looked cross. And the King… Oh, no. The King looked like thunder.

"What is going on down here?" the Queen asked. "Jake, why have you got leaves in your hair? Why are your fingernails so filthy? And what on earth do you think you're doing, messing around in the dungeons when you should be in bed?"

"We were worried sick when you weren't in your rooms!" the King exploded, his eyebrows low over his eyes, like great hairy caterpillars. "And we managed to drag the truth from Petunia – that you were mucking about down here again!"

"Did she tell you the bit about her locking me in?" Jake asked. Well, he figured if he and Ned were in trouble over this, he might as well get Petunia told off, too.

"She did," the King growled. "Only because we threatened her with not being able to play in the match tomorrow."

Petunia glared down at the stone floor. "Well, he started it, Dad, dropping that spider down my neck," she protested. "He knows I don't like them, and—"

"That's quite enough," the Queen said. "I'm very disappointed in you, Petunia. And you boys, too. You know better than to come sneaking down here at night!"

"Sorry, Mum," Ned said meekly. "Sorry, Dad."

"But we're all right," Jake put in, before his parents could say anything else. He felt like a superhero after his dungeon adventure. "In fact, you won't believe what's just happened!"

He started to tell them the whole story – how the ghost had appeared, how he'd followed it to escape through the secret tunnel, and how the dog had shown him the treasure.

"Treasure?" Petunia echoed. "You found some treasure?"

A grin broke over Jake's face. He should have guessed that would be the only bit his sister really cared about. "Yes," he said, opening the box to show them. "Look!"

The King read the letter out loud and whistled. "This is incredible!" he cried, the hairy caterpillars shooting right up into his hairline. "What a find!"

"Cool! Can I have the dagger?" Ned asked, brandishing it in the air.

"Definitely not," the Queen said, taking it off him at once.

"Ooh," Petunia said, spotting the bracelet. "Look, Mum!"

"Oh!" the Queen gasped. "A matching bracelet! Isn't that amazing?"

"Yeah, good, isn't it?" Jake said. He polished it with his pyjama sleeve, then clipped it onto his arm. "Think it suits me?" he laughed.

Petunia looked longingly at it, then turned her eyes to Jake. "Jake," she said slowly. "I was wondering... You know I was trying to find a lucky charm for the polo match tomorrow?"

"Ye-e-es," Jake said, holding the bracelet up to the light so that it shone.

"Well," Petunia went on, "it would be really, really nice of you if you let me... borrow the bracelet as my lucky charm?"

Jake was silent. Excellent! A bit of power over his big sister – what a result! "What's the magic word?" he asked after a moment.

"Please?" Petunia added, through gritted teeth.

73

Jake tipped his head to one side,
pretending to consider the question.
"Maybe," he said. "I'll think about it.
But Petunia…"

"Yes?" she asked eagerly.

"You'll have to do some MAJOR
grovelling and begging first," Jake told
her, dropping the bracelet in his pyjama
pocket. He grinned. In one evening,
he'd pulled off Ned's dare, met a ghost,

found some treasure, and now he had
Petunia's sucking-up to look forward
to. Oh, he did love it when everything
turned out perfectly!

LOOK OUT FOR MORE
RIGHT ROYAL LAUGHS WITH

Sticky Gum Fun
978 1 40830 276 7   £8.99

It's Snow Joke!
978 1 40830 277 4   £8.99

Dungeon of Doom
978 1 40830 280 4   £8.99

Knighty-Knight
978 1 40830 281 1   £8.99

Monster Madness
978 1 40830 278 1   £8.99

Swordfights and Slimeballs!
978 1 40830 279 8   £8.99

Here's a taster of

Knighty-Knight

CRACK!

Prince Jake's cue ball smashed straight into the pack of red balls, sending them scattering all over the king-sized snooker table. It was a Thursday evening, and the Moranian royal family were in the games room, over in the east wing of their castle. "Yes!" Jake whooped, jumping up and punching the air as the white ball came to rest behind the brown. "You are totally snookered, Dad!"

King Nicholas walked thoughtfully around the snooker table, chalking his cue.

The Queen and Princess Petunia promptly sprinted after him.

"I think you need to hit the cushion *here*," Queen Caroline said, pointing at a spot on the side of the snooker table. "Then you can pot *this* red ball."

"No, Mum," argued Princess Petunia, who was Jake's big sister and thought she knew everything. "If he gets the white to rebound from *here*, he can really stuff Jake for his next shot."

"Oi!" Jake cried indignantly. "Whose side are you on, anyway?"

"Don't worry, Jake," said Prince Ned, who was the youngest of the royal children, and currently playing pinball at the far end of the room. "Dad won't win. Dad never wins at anything."

"Hey, I heard that, you cheeky prince," the King grumbled. "That's no way to speak to a king, thank you very much!"

The King paced around the table once more, then crouched low over it, carefully positioning his snooker cue and closing one eye as he took aim. Jake blinked as his view of the table was suddenly obscured by his dad's rather large bottom. He had to really, REALLY resist the urge to give his dad a sharp prod with his own cue. It was so tempting...

But at that moment, there was a pattering sound...and then a whole chunk of the ceiling came loose, crashing right onto the middle of the snooker table with a mighty THUMP!

Jake blinked. Petunia squealed. And King Nicholas jumped, sending his cue skidding along the cloth and tearing it with a loud *rrrrriiiip*!

The cue ball went spinning across the table, bounced off the lump of plaster and rolled into a side pocket.

Jake grinned as plaster dust drifted down onto the King like snow. Talk about timing! "Oh dear!" he chortled, sliding his marker along five points on the scoreboard. "Unlucky, Dad!"

PICK UP A COPY OF

Knighty-Knight

TO FIND OUT WHAT HAPPENS NEXT!

The *Prince Jake* books are available from all good bookshops,
or can be ordered direct from the publisher:
Orchard Books, PO BOX 29, Douglas IM99 1BQ.
Credit card orders please telephone 01624 836000 or fax 01624 837033 or visit our
website: www.orchardbooks.co.uk or e-mail: bookshop@enterprise.net for details.
To order please quote title, author and ISBN and your full name and address.
Cheques and postal orders should be made payable to 'Bookpost plc.'
Postage and packing is FREE within the UK
(overseas customers should add £2.00 per book).
Prices and availability are subject to change.